That's My Dog

LABRADOR RETRIEVERS

by Tammy Gagne

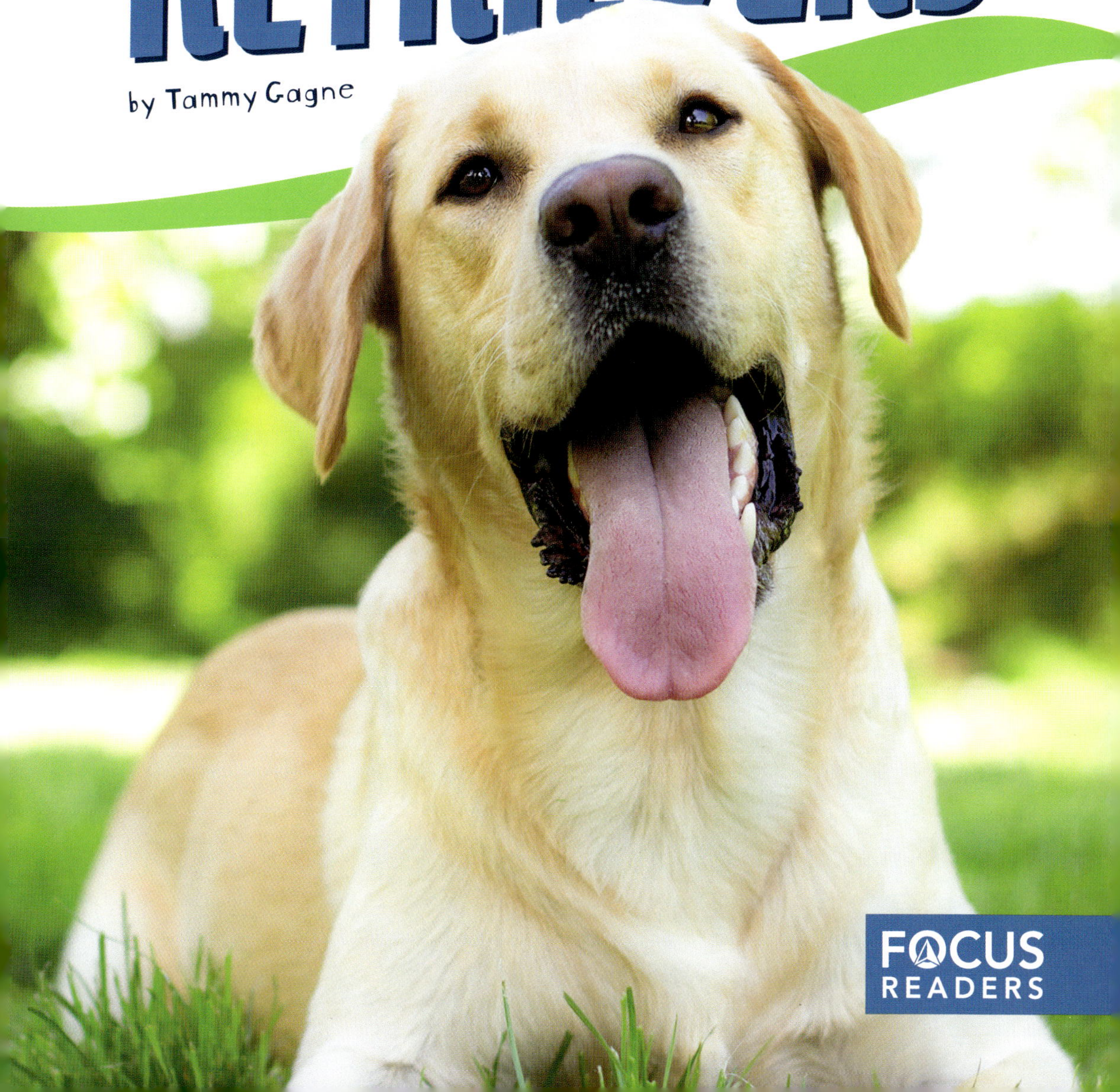

FOCUS READERS

FOCUS READERS

www.focusreaders.com

Focus Readers is distributed by North Star Editions:
sales@northstareditions.com | 888-417-0195

Produced for Focus Readers by Red Line Editorial.

Photographs ©: sanjagrujic/iStockphoto, cover, 1; pliona/iStockphoto, 4–5, 29; People Images/iStockphoto, 6; Julia Zara/Shutterstock Images, 8–9; DenGuy/iStockphoto, 10; RichLegg/iStockphoto, 13; anetapics/Shutterstock Images, 14–15; Rosa Jay/Shutterstock Images, 16; sobaka77/Shutterstock Images, 19; Gerald Marella/Shutterstock Images, 20–21; Thepalmer/iStockphoto, 22–23; Antonio Diaz/iStockphoto, 24; Joesboy/iStockphoto, 27

ISBN
978-1-63517-542-4 (hardcover)
978-1-63517-614-8 (paperback)
978-1-63517-758-9 (ebook pdf)
978-1-63517-686-5 (hosted ebook)

Library of Congress Control Number: 2017948118

Printed in the United States of America
Mankato, MN
November, 2017

About the Author

Tammy Gagne has written more than 150 books for adults and children. She resides in northern New England with her husband and son. One of her favorite pastimes is visiting schools to talk to kids about the writing process.

TABLE OF CONTENTS

CHAPTER 1

MEET THE LABRADOR RETRIEVER

The Labrador retriever is a pleasant companion. It is also a talented working dog. It is often called a Lab. The Labrador **breed** began in Canada. But people everywhere love them.

Labs are known for being great with kids.

Some Labs are therapy dogs. They comfort people.

Labs are one of the most popular breeds in the world. Labrador retrievers are friendly and smart. These traits make Labs great working dogs. Labs can be trained to hunt. They can guide the blind.

Police departments sometimes use Labs to sniff out criminals, too. The Lab's strong sense of smell makes this breed a great detective.

Labs love people of all ages. They are great dogs for families with kids. This breed is gentle and loyal. These characteristics make it an ideal pet.

FUN FACT

Labrador retrievers love water. Many will even jump into puddles.

CHAPTER 2

A BREED FROM CANADA

The Labrador retriever breed began in Newfoundland, Canada. Small dogs lived on this large island in the 1700s. They were strong swimmers. Hunters used them to retrieve **game**.

Today, many owners still take their Labs hunting.

Newfoundland dogs are very large.

Newfoundland dogs were another dog breed on the island. People **crossed** the small dogs with the Newfoundlands. Their puppies were the first Labrador retrievers.

Early Labs helped fishermen. The dogs pulled nets out of the water. They also caught fish that escaped from fishing lines. Later, people crossed Labs with other breeds. These dogs included other retrievers, setters, and spaniels.

FUN FACT

The first Labrador retrievers were named after the city of St. John's in Newfoundland. They were called St. John's water dogs.

These crosses made the Lab's retrieving **instinct** even stronger.

The United Kingdom's Kennel Club (KC) and the American Kennel Club (AKC) are dog registries. These organizations educate the public about dog ownership. The KC recognized the Labrador retriever in 1903. The AKC followed in 1917.

FUN FACT

At dog shows, judges look for Labs with "kind" and "friendly" eyes.

Labs can be trained to help police officers catch criminals.

Later, the breed became popular with hunters. By the 1960s, the Lab was a popular pet.

CHAPTER 3

THE LOOK OF A LAB

Labrador retrievers are strong. These dogs have **muscular** bodies. Their muscles help them run, jump, and swim. Labs have wide heads. Their powerful jaws are useful for retrieving game.

Labs often swim to retrieve game that their owners hunt.

Black, yellow, and chocolate Labs share many similar features.

Labs come in three colors. These dogs may be black, yellow, or chocolate. Black and yellow Labs usually have black noses. Chocolate Labs have brown noses.

All Labs have double coats. This means they have two layers of hair. The outer layer is short and **repels** water. The Lab's inner layer, or undercoat, is thick. This hair keeps the dog warm when it gets wet.

Male Labs are approximately 23 inches (58 cm) tall. They weigh approximately 73 pounds (33 kg).

FUN FACT

The color of a chocolate Lab used to be called liver.

Females are usually smaller. They stand approximately 22 inches (56 cm) tall. Females weigh approximately 63 pounds (29 kg).

The Labrador retriever has an otter tail. This means the tail is thick and strong. The otter tail helps the dog move through the water when swimming. It also helps a Lab keep its balance when walking.

Most Lab puppies reach their adult size in 18 months.

THAT'S AMAZING!

RIVER RESCUE

In 2017, a daring yellow Lab saved a black Lab's life. The two dogs were playing with a large stick. Suddenly, the black Lab fell into a river. The rushing **current** quickly began pulling him under. He struggled to stay afloat. But he did not let go of the stick in his mouth. The yellow Lab on shore then grabbed the other end of the stick. He used it to pull his friend to safety. The black Lab climbed out onto a nearby rock. Neither dog was injured in the accident. A video of the amazing rescue became popular online.

It is important to watch Labs while they are swimming.

CHAPTER 4

CARING FOR A LAB

Caring for a Lab requires some knowledge and work. Labs have short coats. Even dogs with short coats need grooming. Owners should brush their Labs once a week to remove dead hair.

Labs need baths only when they get really dirty. Bathing them too often can make their skin dry.

Owners must watch how much their Labs eat.

Brushing also helps keep the dog clean.

Labrador retrievers can eat a lot. **Obesity** is a common problem for this breed. Overweight dogs are more likely to develop health problems. Owners must be careful not to give Labs too many treats. It is better to reward a Lab with exercise and play time.

Daily exercise also helps Labs stay healthy and use their energy.

FUN FACT

Owners can check their Labs for obesity by feeling for their ribs. If an owner can feel the ribs easily, the dog is probably a healthy weight.

Swimming is one of their favorite activities. But they also enjoy running and playing games such as fetch.

A Lab can live in a house or an apartment. A big yard is a great place for play. Labs can also get exercise at a dog park or the beach.

FUN FACT

Many Labs compete in a sport called dock jumping. This breed can jump as far as 27 feet (8.2 m).

A Lab competes in a dock jumping competition.

FOCUS ON

LABRADOR RETRIEVERS

Write your answers on a separate piece of paper.

1. Write a sentence that describes the key ideas from Chapter 2.
2. What kinds of games would you like to play with a Labrador retriever? Why?
3. Which color do Labrador retrievers not come in?
   - A. black
   - B. gray
   - C. yellow
4. What might happen if a Lab doesn't get enough exercise?
   - A. The dog may become lazy.
   - B. The dog may itch.
   - C. The dog may gain weight.

5. What does **grooming** mean in this book?

*Even dogs with short coats need **grooming**. Owners should brush their Labs once a week to remove dead hair.*

- **A.** to be fed and given water
- **B.** cleaning and caring for
- **C.** exercise and play time

6. What does **characteristics** mean in this book?

*This breed is gentle and loyal. These **characteristics** make it an ideal pet.*

- **A.** physical looks
- **B.** sounds and actions
- **C.** personality traits

Answer key on page 32.

GLOSSARY

breed
A group of animals that share the same looks and features.

crossed
Bred two types of dogs together to produce a new type.

current
The motion of a flowing waterway.

dog shows
Competitions where different dogs are judged based on the standard for their breed.

game
Animals hunted for food or sport.

instinct
A behavior that is natural instead of learned.

muscular
Having a strong and powerful body.

obesity
The condition of being severely overweight.

repels
Resists or pushes away.

TO LEARN MORE

BOOKS

Gagne, Tammy. *Spaniels, Retrievers, and Other Sporting Dogs*. Mankato, MN: Capstone Press, 2017.

Newman, Aline Alexander, and Gary Weitzman. *How to Speak Dog: A Guide to Decoding Dog Language*. Washington, DC: National Geographic, 2013.

Rustad, Martha E. H. *Labrador Retrievers.* Mankato, MN: Amicus, 2018.

NOTE TO EDUCATORS

Visit **www.focusreaders.com** to find lesson plans, activities, links, and other resources related to this title.

INDEX

Answer Key: 1. Answers will vary; **2.** Answers will vary; **3.** B; **4.** C; **5.** B; **6.** C